Corralling the Cowboy

Covet the Cowboy Series, Episode 1

An Erotic Short Story
By

Katie O'Connor

Corralling the Cowboy

Covet the Cowboy Series, Episode 1

Text and Cover Copyright © 2012
Snarky Heart
Press and Katie O'Connor
E-book ISBN: 978-0-988-1281-0-1
Print ISBN: 978-1-7752233-5-1

Dedication

It takes a wild imagination to create a work of fiction, but no story is created without the help of many minds and a few talented hands. Special thanks go to Steena Holmes for her fabulous cover. She saw the images in my mind and made them real.

Kudos to my editors and critics: Phaedra, Deb, Wendy, Carrie, and Betty who gave me much needed feedback and thousands of corrections. Any mistakes left are mine alone.

To my husband for always being there for me, for supporting me and for not divorcing me for yelling "Can ya just shut up, I'm trying to write."

And to the boys of Prague whose macho games provided me a lot of insight into the twisted male persona. Boys, you amuse and inspire me.

Thank each and every one of you! Words alone will never be enough to express my gratitude! Hugs to you all!

Buffalo Days
Rodeo and Celebration

Joe watched her enter the beer garden and look around. She was different from the usual buckle bunny that crowded into the tent, drooling over all the wanna be cowboys. She had an air that set her apart; she seemed … almost like she didn't really want to be there. She moved with a purpose, definitely a woman on a mission. Joe took a moment to study her. Her full lips turned up just a bit at the corner. Her black cowboy hat tilted just a little to the left, almost hiding her eye. Her boots were black and brushed against her calves and for a moment he envied them. Those long, lean legs were made to wrap around a man's waist and pull him closer. His eyes traced the sweet line of her legs from the top of her boots to the hem of her short, tight, black denim skirt. Damn, was there anything sexier than a fit woman in cowboy boots? She pivoted from left to right as she strolled between the tables, looking for someone.

Joe watched her progress, delighting in the brief glimpses of the curve of her ass as she danced her way through the crowd. Her long blonde hair swishing across her shoulders as she moved and he wanted to wrap his hands in it and pull her close. The need to get closer compelled him to move in her direction.

Alex paused just inside the door of the beer garden. Country music pounded loudly in her ears, the beat infectious, making her hips twitch and sway. Thankfully it was late and it wasn't as crowded as it might have been earlier. With the late evening crowd thinning her search for her missing friend would be that much easier. Where the hell had Janine gotten to? She was supposed to give Alex a ride home. Pausing for a moment, Alex turned in a circle, studying the people filling the beer garden; across the tent she spotted some friends. Slowly making her way towards the small group, she kept her eyes open for Janine.

She greeted the group, pausing with her hand on Mick's shoulder, she bent over to be heard over the rowdy country band at the front of the tent. "Hey, guys, has anybody seen Janine? I've been looking for her for nearly an hour."

"I saw her wrapped up in some cowboy's arms earlier," Mandy quipped. "Typical Janine."

"Geez. Again?" Alex groaned. "Can't she just quit with the men already? I swear the girl has no shame at all. The rodeo comes to town and she goes cowboy crazy. Every year she ditches me for some cowboy. I never learn." She twisted her lips thoughtfully. "She was my ride home. What the hell do I do now? Is anyone heading out soon?" She asked. When they all responded negatively, she shook her head and sighed. "I guess I'll take the bus. Well, later guys, I'm gone. I've had enough rodeo and midway for one day." With a wave and a backwards glance at her friends she headed towards the door and collided with a solid wall of flesh.

"Oof." She blinked rapidly and stared at the wide expanse of chest in front of her. A large hand gripped her shoulder, steadying her. Alex tipped her head up and looked into the deepest chocolate brown eyes she had ever seen; she swallowed hard and took an unsteady step backwards.

"Watch yourself Little Lady; you could have knocked me down." He tipped his hat back, his brown eyes twinkling. "You nearly spilled my beer." He gestured towards her with his half empty glass.

Alex couldn't help but smile at his roguish grin. "I think not." She gave him a light push on the chest. He stayed rock solid. "You're much bigger than I am." Her voice cracked and moistened her suddenly dry lips. "Your beer is safe from me." She looked him up and down. He was a tall one. His dark brown cowboy hat matched his boots and tan jeans. His snap front shirt was unbuttoned enticingly at the neck. Oh my, she thought. He is handsome, so big and strong looking, so much more of a man than the typical male at the office where she worked. She wouldn't mind spending time basking in his enticing smile and bulky body. Suddenly, she wasn't all that tired and the rodeo had regained its appeal.

"In fact," she quipped. "I think you probably owe me a beer, for the bruising I'll have where you rammed into me." She winked at him. Wow; where had that come from? She had never hit on a stranger like that before. She tended towards shy, or at least no quite so brazen, but this guy was hot. Way hot. Steaming, smoking and totally lick-ably sexy.

Mr. Tall, broad, and handsome smiled down at her, tipped his hat and offered his hand. "Joe Brooks, at your service. May I buy you a beer to facilitate the repair of the grievous damage I have so callously inflicted on your delicate person?" He asked with mock formality and a small bow.

Oh, she liked a man that could tease her back, and she loved a man with brains. "I'm Alex. Pleased to meet you Joe." His large hand engulfed hers; the rough callouses on the tips of his fingers and palm scratched pleasantly against her soft hand. Joe had a body to die for too. Brains, a sweet smile and a hot body: he might be the perfect man. She was suddenly swamped with images of being in his bed, steaming up the sheets. Oh my! Longing rushed through her. It had been a long time since she wanted a man at first glance, but Joe's smile and solid body made her pulse race.

"Just-Alex?" He asked. "No last name?" He winked at her.

"No last name, a girl needs a little mystery," she answered easily. "But a beer would be lovely." Anything to spend more time with you. She wondered where this flirty side had come from.

He led her to the bar and handed her a glass of draft. "A toast to you Just-Alex, and my apologies for running you down." He raised his glass and bumped it gently against hers.

"You are forgiven and thank you for the beer," she responded with a smile. Looking up at him, she decided that she liked the way he towered over her. He was broad shouldered and strong looking, and there was kindness and laughter in his eyes. "What brought you to Buffalo Days today?" She asked, trying to start a conversation but unsure where to begin.

"Bull riding." He laughed at the shocked look on her face. "I don't ride them; I just admire the skill involved. I have a small ranch and raise some cattle. Livestock is my life." He shrugged. "What brings you here?"

She let him change the subject. She didn't really want to talk anyway; she would rather touch his arms and see if his biceps were a rock hard as they looked. "I came with a friend to watch the chuck wagons and check out the midway, we do it every year." She placed her hand on his arm. It was as hard as it looked and her insides shivered.

"I'm not keeping you from her, am I?" He ran a finger down her arm. "It is a her, right?"

For a moment, Alex forgot to answer him. "Um, yes, she's a girl. A woman. But no, you aren't keeping me from her, we're meeting up later." It wasn't quite the truth, but she really didn't know Joe, and despite his kind eyes, she didn't really want him to know that she suspected she had been abandoned by her friend. Again.

6

"Good to know." He smiled and winked at her. "I'm not quite ready to let you go yet. Tell me something about the life of Just-Alex. What do you do when you're not spending time with your friends at the rodeo?"

"Nothing glamorous, I'm just an office manager. But I do enjoy my work. It keeps my mind busy, and I love the people. I've worked other jobs, but the best part of this one is that at the end of the day, I can go home and leave it all behind." She couldn't get her mind off his body. "You look like you do something physical with all those muscles." Oh god, why had she said that. He would think she was ogling him.

He laughed and gave her a quick one-armed hug. "Good guess, I do physical work for a good part of the day. I love being outdoors. I don't think I could be trapped in an office all day. But to each his own."

His arm brushed her shoulder sending a wave of heat through Alex. His body was hot in the cooling air inside the large beer garden tent; as if his body had absorbed the heat of the sun and he was passing that heat onto her. Alex stifled a smile at the whimsical thought. It was body heat, nothing more, but oh what a body. She leaned into him a bit, absorbing his warmth and flirting just a little.

They talked about the headline band that had performed on the outdoor stage earlier, a favorite of them both. "My sister thinks the lead singer is the hottest man on earth," Joe told her with a laugh. "I just think he needs a haircut, even if he does have a talented voice."

Alex laughed. "He has great eyes, but it's all I can do not to climb onto the stage and cut his hair. I'm not a long-hair-on-men kind of girl. I like it short and tidy."

Joe lifted his hat to reveal his short, well-trimmed brown hair with a mild case of hat-hair. "I'm a short hair man myself. Although I expect that after an entire day in this hat, my hair is anything but tidy." He winked at her and reached out to tug gently on a lock of hair hanging over her shoulder. "And I love long hair on women. Especially blonde hair." His words were a blatant come on.

He winked again and her knees went weak. It was a good thing she hand her arm on his forearm or she would have fallen. He had the strangest effect on her body. She felt tingly and alive, like she was waiting for something special. Something only he could give her.

"What's your favorite ride?" He asked suddenly.

For a moment, she pictured herself astride him, then realized that wasn't the kind of ride he had in mind. She swallowed hard. "The Ferris Wheel," she answered with a laugh. "Janine loves the real wild rides, but I'm a bit of a chicken. But the view from the top can't be beat." They talked about the midway, the rides, the games and the crazy food for a while.

"Drink up, and I'll take you for a spin on the Ferris Wheel." Joe drained his glass and indicated that she should finish hers too. "It's getting dark and everything will shut down soon, but I think the lights will be amazing from the top right now." He waved a handful of ride tickets under her nose. "I love the rides," he confessed with a sheepish grin. She grinned back and they headed for the wheel. The line was blessedly short and they were skyward in minutes. They enjoyed the ride enough that when they reached the bottom, they handed over more tickets and went for another round. Twice.

It was nearly full dark, and their car stopped at the top of the Ferris wheel. They sat swaying and enjoying the lights as the evening continued to darken around them. The evening had a feel of fun and frivolity, and the expectation of something

9

exciting to come. An occasional a bark of laughter jumped out of the background of tinkling carnival noises. The moon was nearly full, casting its light over everything and pushing the falling darkness back. "It's beautiful, isn't it?" She asked, looking down at the lights of the midway and the city.

"Yes, it is," he said with a catch in his voice.

When she looked at him, he wasn't looking at the lights, he was staring at her. Joe slid his arm around her shoulders and pulled her close to his side. His breath was soft in her hair, his fingers gentle but firm as he tipped her face up to look at him. Oh my, she thought, I wasn't expecting this.

"I'm going to kiss you," he warned softly, leaning slowly towards her.

"I hardly know you," she responded, tilting her head to the left, wordlessly inviting him in. His lips brushed, featherlike, across hers. She shivered and pushed back against him, deepening the contact. She had been aroused since she bumped into him in the beer garden. Now, she wanted him with a desire that shocked her. Something about this man called to her, sending a pulse of longing racing through her to lodge in her core.

"Kiss me again," she whispered against his lips. She cupped his face between her hands and pulled him closer, pressing her mouth against his. She obeyed without question when he cupped her head and kissed her deeply, demanding she respond in kind. She wanted this, needed it. Her hands dropped to his shoulders and she explored the rock-hard muscles there, tracing each contour and line with her fingers. His arms were like rocks and the sheer power of him was almost overwhelming. Joe's hand cupped her breast and the Ferris wheel gave a small jerk and started its slow descent, jerking her back to reality.

Oh, she thought, I should be resisting this. They were in public, high above the thinning midway crowd and she knew nothing about this man except his name, if Joe Brooks was his real name. Even as the thought formed, she rejected it. Somehow, she was sure he wasn't lying to her. She felt something new here, and she wanted this, wanted him. It wasn't like her to be this attracted to a stranger, but the atmosphere, the beer, and Joe were an overpowering combination and she didn't want to resist. She wasn't going to resist. She was going to take everything he offered.

He stroked his palm lightly across her breast, and they moaned in unison when her nipple pebbled against his hand. "I want you Alex," he whispered against her mouth.

She whimpered and arched her back, pushing her breast against his palm. Her hands ranged everywhere, eager to explore every taut muscle of his body. His body was different from the typical man she dated. Joe was definitely used to physical work, and Alex usually dated suit and tie types who kept in shape by making large monthly payments to the local gym. She decided she liked his tight, hard shape with all its muscles and heat.

Alex was startled when the ride attendant cleared his throat. "Last stop folks," he said with a laugh. "Ride's over, I'm shutting 'er down for the night."

Chagrinned, Alex allowed Joe to take her hand and lead her down the ramp and back onto the midway. The people were few and far between, only the diehard rodeo and midway fans remained. It wouldn't be long before security starting shooing people home. Alex and Joe strolled through the booths, hand in hand listening to the banter of the carnies and laughter of the few remaining guests. A few of the games and food booths were already shut down. As they walked, his thumb stroked her palm and her wrist, sending her mind whirling to thoughts of what those talented hands would feel like on other parts of her body. Her naked body.

"Hang on for a second," Alex told Joe and darted into the washroom. She needed to use the washroom, but more than that, she needed a few minutes to recoup her equilibrium. A minute later, she stood before the sink staring at her flushed face. *Damn, look at me. I'm flushed and definitely look like I've been well and thoroughly kissed.* If that ride had been any longer, she knew that more than her hair would have been in disarray and probably would never have seen her cowboy hat again. She would have let Joe lead her where ever he wanted. Strangely, the idea didn't distress her; it thrilled her. She studied herself for another minute and decided she liked the well-kissed look, smoothed her hair, plunked her hat back on and turned to leave.

Stopping in her tracks, Alex wondered how far Joe would take this. She hoisted up her short skirt and whisked off her panties and stuffed them into her skirt pocket. As she straightened she noticed a grey-haired woman standing just inside the doorway, grinning broadly at her.

"Go get him, Sweetie. He'll never know what hit him." The woman laughed and entered a stall leaving Alex staring at her back.

"What the heck," Alex said with a laugh. "Nothing ventured, nothing gained. Wish me luck," she called over her shoulder towards the stall; then she sucked in a calming breath, squared her shoulders and strode outside to join Joe. He was leaning against the side of the building waiting for her, a patient smile on his face.

"Thought you got lost," he teased.

"Nope," she gave him a naughty grin. "Just lost these," she dangled her panties in front of him.

"What is that?" He asked, his hand darting out and snatching them from her. He held up the tiny lace panties between his large rough hands and looked at them before glancing at her with a raised eyebrow. "Geez, do you always wear panties this sexy?"

Alex laughed. "I do, and always with a matching bra. I have a huge lingerie collection." She winked at him, laughing when he groaned.

Joe stuffed the panties into his jeans pocket, snaked his hand out to cup the back of her head and draw her close. "You

14

are a naughty girl," he declared, with a smile, tugging her forward and kissing her.

A shiver of delight raced through her, this was what she wanted, what she needed. A quick fling, a one-night stand. It wasn't something she had ever thought she would enjoy, but right now, with this man; the thought alone was making her pussy feel wet and throbbing. She wasn't sure she could resist the temptation, wasn't sure she even wanted to resist. She slid her hands up his chest and around his neck, and leaned into him. Pressing her full length against him, she kissed him back. It was like pressing against a brick wall. He was solid and warm. The kiss was rough and urgent and her knees went weak.

Joe's ran his hands over her back to stroke the curve of her hips and the narrowing of her waist. Her muscles twitched under his hand. He wanted Alex, here now, hard, fast and without any preliminaries. And unless he missed his guess, she wanted him just and badly. Hell, she had almost thrown her panties in his face, if that wasn't a sign that she was into him, he didn't know what was. He traced the contours of her waist, and slid his hands along her arms to where her hands were locked behind his neck.

The heat of his hands-on Alex's back, on her arms was enough to burn her, to drive her desire higher. Fire followed his touch and she wiggled against him, trying to get closer, to get inside him. Joe's hands gripped her wrists lightly and in one quick motion he turned them, so her back was against the wall, her hands pinned above her head.

Breaking their kiss, he paused and looked down at her. She went still for a second, and he felt her relax when he smiled softly at her. He studied her eyes, and her face; reading no objection there, lowered his mouth to kiss the column of her neck.

The building pressed into her back, the rough wood siding hard and unyielding. Their cowboy hats were knocked askew and tumbled to the ground but she didn't care. Joe's long, hard body pressed against her and he held her wrists pinned lightly over her head with one hand. Her breath caught in her throat when his lips touched her neck and her body burned for more. She pushed her hips forward, bumping against his erection. His obvious need made her heart pound, and her breath flew out in a rush. She twisted her wrists in his hand and he loosened his grip just enough that she knew she could break free if she really wanted to. But there was something so hot, so erotic, and arousing about being trapped that she let him hold her there, and ground her hips against him. Her hips bumped his and he pressed back, pinning her entire length against the wall, his cock was hard against her belly leaving no doubt that he wanted her as badly as she wanted him.

Who would ever have guessed that she had an exhibitionist side or that she would enjoy being at the mercy of a man? But she would be damned if she wasn't completely into this and eager for more. His lips were soft on her neck sending heat racing through her. His free hand stroked her side and stole under her shirt to explore her bare skin. His hand was hot and the late evening air cool. She shivered in delight and moaned loudly. She tried to kiss his neck, to taste him, but he eased back a touch, keeping away from her eager mouth.

"Slow down," he whispered; his breath hot against her skin. "I want to taste you first." He dipped his head back to her neck and kissed along the column of her neck and down along the upper curve of her breast.

"Kiss me," she begged.

"I am kissing you," he said with a laugh.

She groaned low in her throat. "On the mouth. I need to kiss you," she begged. "Please."

Joe straightened up and looked into her eyes. "Begging?" He teased and brushed his lips softly across hers. "I like that."

Alex pressed towards him, trying to deepen the light contact, but he moved back.

"What do you want?" He asked; his hand busy exploring her stomach and waist, her skin was as soft as the finest silk and hot under his touch. "Tell me what you want Alex."

"Kiss me. Please." She pleaded softly.

"Is that the best you can do?" He asked, nibbling on her ear.

"Oh god, Joe. Kiss me, hard. I need to taste you, to kiss you." She didn't care that she was begging. She twisted her head, trying to capture his mouth. She was burning for him.

"My, my, my. That's my girl. We are eager, aren't we?" He teased before swooping in and capturing her mouth with his.

She kissed him hard, urgently, giving and taking. Her teeth scraped his lip, nibbled gently and she soothed the tiny

18

hurt with her tongue. She groaned into his mouth, her breath coming in gasps, her heart pounding, her pussy aching. She lost herself in him, in his scent, his taste and in the feel of being at his mercy.

The sound of a woman's giggle brought them to their senses. They broke apart and Alex saw the woman from the bathroom walking away.

"Holy hell," Alex whispered. "I forgot where we were."

"Come on." Joe scooped their hats up from the ground and tugged on her arm, moving towards the back of the building. "Let's find somewhere more private. "I'm not finished with you yet." When she didn't immediately move, he gave her a light swat on the bottom. "Are you coming?" He looked down at her, giving her the chance to walk away, to stop what was happening between them.

The smack to her behind got Alex moving, she hurried around the building, almost dragging Joe behind her. She wasn't sure what had gotten into her, but she wasn't ready to leave him yet, his touch was electric and she needed more of it. She paused, but Joe pulled her further into the shadows, away from the lights of the midway and into the darkness between two buildings. The chatter of the depleting crowd faded as they moved farther from the midway. The sound of the carnival rides and games dimmed until it was nothing but white noise with an occasional jolt of laughter breaking through. Although the celebrations continued unchecked only a hundred yards away, it felt like Alex and Joe had stepped into their own private world.

"Come here," he said his voice soft and commanding. He tossed their hats on a plastic patio chair abandoned behind the building.

Alex obeyed without a thought and stepped into his arms. He embraced her and pivoted quickly so she was once again pressed against the wall, her hands pinned above her head. This time he didn't give her the opportunity to object. He just ravaged her mouth, kissing her hard and deep, demanding she respond. She kissed him back, giving and taking, playing along with him eager for more. Her body was throbbing, aching.

Would he take her here? Now? Would she let him? Alex decided she didn't care and gave herself up to the moment, taking all he had to give.

Her buttons flew open under his nimble fingers. His touch was soft, gentle where he traced the line of skin revealed by his actions and Alex inhaled sharply as his palm grazed across her breast, the light contact drawing the soft lace across her nipple. Shivers raced thought her and her nipple peaked, hard. It felt like it was trying to force its way through the thin lace of her bra.

"Your nipple is like a rock." He murmured into her neck. "Is the other one as hard as this one?" He flicked his thumb back and forth across one, kissed his way to the other, took it between his teeth and nibbled sharply.

It felt exquisite and Alex bucked against him, thrusting her breast against his mouth, trying to get him to take her nipple further into his mouth. She needed to be closer, to crawl inside him, to become one with him. No, she needed him inside her. Her body ached for his, with a burning need that was almost frightening in its intensity.

His mouth was like a brand, scalding her breasts as he teased them through her bra. He flicked its front clasp open and then dropped his hand to her thigh. Slowly he inched her skirt upwards, snaking his hand underneath. He grunted his approval when his hand met naked thigh above the top of her stocking. His fingers traced higher and higher, his mouth pushed the lace cup of her bra off one breast and then the other. He moved back and forth between them, nibbling, kissing, and teasing Alex.

His fingers met her naked mound and he jerked back in surprise and looked at her. "Stockings, and no hair. Geez. You're so smooth." He delved deeper. "And so wet."

He sounded breathless, like he was in agony and Alex smiled up at him. "I need you," she confessed, pushing her hips against his questing hand. "Touch me," she begged. The burning need encompassing her left no room for pride. She was a crazy with need for his touch.

One finger slid inside and he teased her clit with his thumb. "Babe," he whispered against her breast. He was hunched over awkwardly to reach her breast with his mouth while he pressed her hands above her head with one hand and toyed with her wetness with the other. He didn't care about the kink in his back; all he wanted was to have this woman. To take her here, now and to take her hard.

She felt her pussy clenched against his finger as he eased it slowly in and out. After a few long slow strokes he added another finger, moving his hand faster, timing his motions to the thrusts of her hips, pressing the heel of his hand against her clit with each stroke. Her breathing was harsh, her heart pounding, her blood felt like it was boiling and shivers wracked her body. Damn, she was going to come. Already. She had only known this man for an hour and he already had her on the brink of orgasm, as if their bodies had known one another for a lifetime.

"Oh. Yes. Please," she whimpered. She felt almost abandoned when Joe's mouth left her breast as he straightened up to look down at her. Nobody had ever watched her orgasm before; her face flushed hot with embarrassment and she closed her eyes.

"Look at me," he commanded softly. "Your pleasure is beautiful. I want to see you come." His thumb danced across her clit as he stroked slowly in and out of her.

"Harder, oh god, harder. Please." She begged, grinding her hips against him, urging him on. Their eyes locked together as her pleasure mounted. It was mortifying and arousing and it was going to drive her over the edge quickly.

"That's it Alex, come for me. Give me your pleasure." She was lovely to watch, even in the dim light of late evening. He could see the sparkle of her eyes in the moonlight, and could tell her face was flushed with excitement. His cock was rock hard and for a brief moment he wondered if he was going to lose it and come in his pants like a teenager. "Come for me," he commanded again.

His demand tipped her over the edge and she ground against his hand, forcing his fingers deep, grinding her clit against the heel of his hand. Her head thrashed back and forth, she tried to keep her eyes open, like he wanted, but couldn't.

"Oh, please," she begged, trying to ask for enough to tip her over the edge. Coherent thought became impossible and she had no words, all she had were feelings, sensations spiraling tighter and tighter. Like a spring coiling tighter and tighter until she uncoiled with a snap and exploded over the end into pleasure.

Alex's heart was still pounding in her ears when she opened her eyes. Joe smiled down at her and winked.

"That was beautiful. You are beautiful." He kissed her on the tip of her nose. Slowly he slid his fingers from her core and brought them to his face. He inhaled deeply and without breaking eye contact slipped one finger, then the other into his mouth, sucking them clean. Alex flushed and dropped her eyes.

"Look at me," Joe commanded softly. "You taste delicious. See for yourself." He lowered his mouth to hers.

She could taste her arousal on his lips; dark, earthy and a bit salty. It was different, but not unpleasant, so she let him kiss her deeply and kissed him back with all the fire and passion she had inside. One orgasm wasn't going to be enough. She needed another one, maybe more than one and she definitely needed him inside of her. Buried balls deep. She didn't know where the words came from, but knew it was what she wanted. Needed. Now.

She fumbled with his belt, then his button-fly. God, who wore full button-flies? Too many buttons, a zipper would have been much easier. She didn't have the patience for this, not now. Finally, the buttons were all free and she shoved his pants to his knees, her fingers grabbing greedily at the rock-hard length beneath his tight boxer briefs. It was enough to make her drool. She squatted before him, and tugged his briefs down. His cock sprang free and tapped her on the nose. She giggled and looked up at him, licking the head of his cock and engulfing it without breaking eye contact. She snorted in amusement when his eyes rolled back into his head.

His cock was huge, almost more than she could wrap her mouth around. There was no way in hell she was going to be able to take the entire length in her mouth. Bracing herself with one hand against his thigh for balance, she wrapped his cock in the other and pumped slowly, bobbing her head, taking as much as she could, flicking the rounded head with her tongue each time she pulled back. He twitched against her mouth, groaning low in his throat. His hands cupped her head, his fingers tangled in her hair, guiding her motions, not controlling, not forceful, just gently showing her what he liked, what he needed. He moved slowly, pumping into her mouth, his thighs clenched under her hand and he moaned.

He tasted good, salty and he smelled like heaven. How could a man smell so good after spending the day in the hot sun and the evening in a beer garden? She didn't care; she inhaled deeply, memorizing his scent, filing it away for later pleasure. His thigh twitched and his hips bucked convulsively against her. He was trying to control himself, she could tell and the rush of power made her smile. Her pussy gushed. Damn she needed him.

Almost as if he were reading Alex's mind, Joe pulled her gently to her feet. "Enough," he moaned and kissed her harshly on the mouth. "I can't take any more without coming."

She smiled against his mouth. "Aw, I feel bad."

"Minx." He laughed with her and backed her against the wall. "Wrap your arms around my neck and your legs around my waist."

She tugged her skirt up and gave a little hop, his hands under her ass helping Alex get high enough to wrap her legs around him. She hugged him tight, burying her face in his neck. Her skirt rode high and his cock bumped against her pussy. "Oh," she moaned, wiggling to align him just right. "There," she pressed down a little and his tip slipped inside her waiting core. "Right there." Her breath rushed out on a sigh of wanting, of impatience.

Slowly, Joe pushed forward, bracing her against the wall, his hands holding her in place. His cock stretched her pussy wide as it inched inside. She tried to push down against him, to hurry him, but every time she moved, he backed away.

"Uh uh," he chided gently "we're taking this slow." He eased in another fraction of an inch, stopping when she tilted her hips down to take in more.

"Now, faster," she begged, trying again to thrust herself down onto him. Joe responded by easing back again, and she forced herself to stay still and let him take the lead. He rewarded her by pumping his hips twice, quickly, slipping another inch inside her. Damn, she wanted to move, needed to move. She needed him deep inside her, desire burned through her like a wildfire, burning, consuming, laying waste to everything but her need to have him. But he was having no part of her urgency.

Joe groaned at the effort it took to maintain control and take this slow. But there was something about Alex that made him want to delay his own release, to be sure she was satisfied, that she came more than once before his took his own pleasure. His need threatened to overwhelm him, to take over his mind as well as his body, but he fought it back. Alex was so sweet, so sexy and so responsive that he wanted to give her his best, even if they were pressed up against the back of a building in the dark corner of the midway.

"Please," she begged again, pressing her mouth against his. She nibbled his lip, loving the hint of beer she found there. How could beer breath be arousing? This whole thing was driving her crazy; she couldn't remember the last time she had been this aroused, this desperate to be fucked. It wasn't just that it had been months since she had sex, it was more than that. It was Joe, it was their location. It was the absolute absurdity of making love outside, in public and taking the risk of being caught.

Fire shot through her when Joe bit her lip and tugged on it gently. He kissed his way to her earlobe and nibbled it gently before tugging on it with his lips. With each tug, he twitched his cock inside her, driving her wild. Her pussy clenched tight, trying to draw him deeper. Her hips twisted and writhed. Her entire body was on fire, burning for Joe, burning for completion.

"Damn," Joe groaned and slammed his cock deep inside her.

"Oh. Yes." Coherent thought was beyond Alex. This felt so good, his cock buried deep, stretching her wide, his pelvis banging against her clit. They stayed motionless for a moment, lost in the sensation of full penetration. His cock twitched inside her, while her pussy gripped and relaxed convulsively around him. Slowly, Joe began to move his hips. Alex wanted to move with him, but she was pinned tight against the wall as he pumped into her slow and deep. All she could do was tilt her hips, improving the angle and increasing the wondrous contact with her groin.

Damn it felt so good, his cock sliding in and out of her, each slow-motion tugging against her clit, teasing and arousing. Her orgasm was building and there was no way she could stop it. She wanted to come with Joe, but couldn't wait for him. This slow pace was as much torture as it was pleasure. She closed her eyes and leaned her head back against the wall, savouring each stroke and the line of fire it sent racing through her.

"Play with your breasts," Joe grunted, stepping back a bit, changing his angle of penetration and making space between their bodies. "Look at me while you do it."

Alex cupped her breasts in her hands, her thumbs stroking back and forth over her nipples in time to Joe's fucking. She opened her eyes and looked at him. His eyes sparkled as he looked down at her.

"God, that looks so incredible," he groaned. "Pinch your nipples for me."

Hot moisture gushed from her pussy, drenching them both as she obeyed his command. She pinched and teased herself, watching his eyes darken in desire. Alex panted and groaned as she pleasured herself, tweaking her nipples just the way she liked it, the way she had when she masturbated during those months of celibacy.

"Harder," she begged, unable to wait any longer for her orgasm. Slow and gentle wasn't working for her, she needed hard and fast. She had waited too long for this. Too many months without a man; too many minutes without Joe. She needed him. Hard.

Joe's pace increased, he pumped harder, faster and each pump banged against her clit, and dug the rough wall into her back. It was pleasure, it was pain, it was fantastic. Tingles raced from her breasts and her pussy, zinging through her body and raising gooseflesh. Her clit throbbed, her heart pounded and her blood raced. Her pussy clenched, gushed and hard throbbing took over her body as her orgasm overcame her.

Distantly she was aware of Joe groaning, his cock throbbing as he reached his own peak, but the sensations swamping her left little room for concern for his pleasure, her entire world was locked in her own body, in her orgasm. Slowly she drifted back down to reality and smiled up at him. "That was fabulous." Her voice was dark with remnants of her desire.

Joe grunted. "Yes, it was." He leaned in to kiss her.

A sudden beam of light bounced off the building beside them and Joe dropped her to her feet and stood between her and the light source.

"You folks okay?" A voice filled with laughter called out of the darkness as the small beam of light played over them.

"Yes. Fine," Joe turned to look at the speaker. "Fuck. It's a security guard," he whispered. "Get dressed and I'll distract him." He fumbled to get his pants back in place; the buttons refastened and turn around without exposing Alex to the guard's view.

"We're fine," he repeated. "Just going to head home," Joe lied.

"Miss, are you alright?" The guard asked, clearly unwilling to leave her with Joe if she didn't want to be there.

"I'm fine." She peeked around Joe's body and waved at the guard, her other hand stayed busy straightening her clothes.

He took a few steps towards them and lowered the flashlight beam. "You folks have to move along," he informed them. "The midway is closed for the night and the rides are all finished. I know how exciting the rodeo can be, but you had best continue this someplace else." He laughed aloud at his own innuendo. "Pick up your hats and I'll walk you to the gate. Before someone comes along and sees you."

Ten minutes later, he shut the park gate behind them and they burst into laughter. "Geez, do you think he saw us?" Alex asked between chagrinned giggles.

"I think he watched the whole damned thing," Joe responded torn between laughter and anger. He pulled Alex into his arms and cupped her cheek softly in his hand. "Sorry about that. I didn't mean to take advantage, or to get us caught. And I sure as hell didn't intend for some perv to watch us. I just can't resist you."

She kissed him deeply. "You gave me plenty of chances to leave.' She buried her face in his shoulder and mumbled, "Besides, the thrill of getting caught was exciting. I just didn't expect to actually be caught."

"Neither did I." He kissed her again. "Can I buy you a drink in compensation for the indignity of getting caught?" It was a poor effort at keeping them together and they both knew it.

It was cute how he returned to the mock formality he had used when they first bumped into each other. Was he nervous? Now? Alex glanced at her watch. "At one thirty in the morning?" She didn't really want to leave him yet so she added. "Your place?"

"I live on a ranch nearly two hours from here, how about yours?" He suggested.

"Um," Alex waffled. She didn't really know him well enough to take him back to her place. She had a policy of not taking strange men home with her and while she didn't usually fuck strange men either, she wasn't about to break another rule, no matter how hot the man was. And Joe was hot. Hot enough that she already wanted him again.

Joe could see that she was uncomfortable with the idea of taking him home. "A hotel?" He asked tentatively. "I like you Alex, and I want to spend more time with you." He lowered his lips to hers, unable to resist the temptation of kissing her again.

Thank god, she thought. I'm not done with you either. Her body still burned with unspent desire. She needed more of this man and she poured every ounce of that desire, that unused passion into her kiss. She pulled his head down against hers, crushing their mouths together, and driving her tongue into his mouth. Their hats fell, unheeded, to the sidewalk. Her hands tangled in his short hair, tugging and guiding their kiss.

He lowered his hands and cupped her ass, lifting her against him, putting their mouths on an even level. His hands wormed their way under her skirt to stroke her soft, naked skin.

The harsh sound of metal banging on metal jarred them back to reality. The security guard was banging his flashlight on the gate. Joe dropped Alex to her feet and she smoothed her skirt down, trying to avoid looking at the guard. She couldn't decide whether she was mortified or amused by the whole thing.

"Move along folks, finish this someplace else. There's a taxi stand half a block down." He stood there, hands on his hips, a big smirk on his face.

Scooping their hats from the ground, Joe placed Alex's on her head and used his to make a sweeping bow towards the guard. "Your wish is our command." Laughing, he took Alex by the hand and led her towards the taxi idling just up the street.

Trapping her body between his own and the taxi, Joe looked down at Alex. "Look," he said, "I don't want to pressure you. If you want to leave I understand." Softly, he traced the line of her cheek with his finger. "I like you Just-

Alex and I want to get to know you better." He fiddled with the brim of his hat with one hand.

"There's a couple of ways to do this," he continued. "I can give you my number, pay for your cab home and let you go. Maybe you'll call me some time. We can't go to my room, I'm room-sharing with an employee. Or we can find a hotel and spend a bit more time together." He wrinkled his brow. "That came out wrong. No pressure there either. Hell, I'll settle for a coffee shop." He shrugged and looked nervous, as if his admission embarrassed him.

Alex placed her hands on his chest and pushed him back a step. Turning, she opened the taxi door and slid inside. She winked up at him. "Are you coming, or are you gonna stand there and jabber all night." She laughed when he tripped in his haste to get into the car. Turning to the cabbie she said, "Where can we find a hotel?"

The cabbie finally convinced them that there was no way they would find a hotel this late at night during Buffalo Days. Every room in the city had been booked for weeks, maybe months. They settled on a quiet all-night coffee shop he recommended. As the taxi pulled away from the curb, Alex cuddled up to Joe's side and rested her head on his chest. His arm snaked around her shoulder, his hand warm against her chilled skin. As the evening had progressed, it had become cool. Wrapped up in their loving, Alex hadn't noticed the chill until she climbed into the cab.

"Oh, you're nice and warm." She wiggled herself closer to his heat.

"Your arm is freezing, you must be cold. I'll warm you up," he said, cupping her chin in his hand and tilting her mouth up to his. He kissed her softly and drew her further into his arms. "Damn you taste good," he whispered against her lips.

He was wrong, Alex thought, she didn't taste good, he did. But he was right about warming her up. Heat rushed through her and she quickly lost the chilled feeling. She snuggled closer and crawled right into his lap, her legs straddled his and his arms were wrapped around her. His hands were hot on her back and arms, his mouth scorching as he kissed his way along her neckline.

She raised her hands to his shoulders, revelling in their width and hard muscles, exploring each curve and hard line. It wasn't enough; she grasped the neckline of his shirt with both hands and yanked it open.

"Good thing it's a snap front shirt," he laughed. "Or all my buttons would be gone."

Alex didn't care; she slid her hands inside the shirt and lowered her mouth to taste him. How could a man taste that good? She nibbled and licked his chest, her tongue teasing his pebbled nipples. He grunted and twisted under her touch and she laughed.

"You're at my mercy now," she said, lightly biting one nipple.

"I think not," Joe said; his hands cupped her breasts, his thumbs stroking back and forth over her nipples.

Shivers wracked her body, darting out from her nipples and lodging in her core. Damn she needed him. Again. Her arms dropped to her sides and she leaned back, exposing herself to him. She wanted to touch him, to explore his body and find all the places she had missed earlier, but his touch left her weak, breathless and unable to do anything but enjoy his caress. She whimpered her surrender. Distantly, she thought she heard the cabbie clear his throat but she was beyond caring. She was desperate for more, to take Joe inside her once again and he had barely touched her.

She had never reacted to a man like this and had chalked it up to the excitement of being with a stranger in public. Now, she wasn't sure that applied. While she didn't really know Joe, she felt safe with him. Why was she so aroused by Joe? Confusion wracked through her and she stiffened on his lap.

"Sh," Joe whispered. "Don't over-think this." He kissed her again and she forgot her objections.

Her short skirt was binding her legs, cutting into them, so Alex yanked it up, heedless and uncaring that her entire ass was exposed. There was something thrilling about exposing herself to Joe while the driver watched. Adjusting her position, she ground herself down against Joe's rock-hard cock through his jeans, loving the way it felt against her wet, open folds. She writhed against him, pumping her hips back and forth, stimulating her clit. Reaching behind her with one hand, she braced it on his knee and gripped his shoulder with other. "Touch me," she urged, pushing her breasts forward as she ground against him.

Joe teased her breasts through the thin fabric of her shirt and bra. With an abrupt motion, he yanked her shirt up and shoved the bra out of the way. He lowered his mouth and

39

sucked her left nipple into his mouth. He teased the nipple with his teeth and tongue before moving on to the right one. He played back and forth between them, building her arousal, fueling his own until he couldn't take it any longer.

Reaching under Alex he fumbled with the multiple buttons of his jeans. Damn, he would never wear a button fly again. Access was just too difficult, especially while keeping his mouth busy on Alex's delectable breasts. He was in a hurry, and a zipper would have been much faster. He fumbled frantically at his buttons, tearing one free in his haste to unfasten it. Uncaring, he dropped the button on the seat.

Alex lifted her weight onto her knees, and shifted backwards, allowing his hands access to his fly. She gripped his head between her hands, tangling her fingers in his short hair, guiding his mouth between her breasts, helping him find the perfect spot, the perfect motion to please her. His mouth felt so damned good against her heated flesh, but she needed more. She felt his hips buck as he yanked his pants down a few inches to expose his cock fully. With a twist and quick jerk of her hips, she encased his cock deep inside her and dropped down to grind against him.

"Finally," she groaned. "Damn that feels good."

40

Joe grunted his agreement and thrust up against her, sinking his cock fully into her moist heat. Heedless of the taxi's motion and the fact the cabbie's attention was divided between their actions and the road, they moved with one another. There was an urgency to their coupling, despite their earlier release. The electricity between them was unmistakable and undeniable.

They rode each other hard and fast. Alex's arousal peaked quickly, her pussy clenching around him as it built. Her fingers dug into his hair and she forced his face upwards. She devoured his mouth and when his tongue tangled with his, her orgasm overcame her and she cried her release against his mouth.

The tight, hard clenching of her pussy around him was more than Joe could bear. Alex's cry of relief tipped Joe over the edge and he slammed into her. Once. Twice. Three times, before exploding into his own world of pleasure and release. Slowly, he eased back to reality and kissed Alex gently on the mouth. His lips were soft as he rained small kisses all over her face and neck.

His gentle kisses pleased Alex and made her feel cherished despite the urgency they had shared. "Damn that was good." She kissed Joe and slid off his lap, pulling her bra back into place. She straightened her shirt and held out her hand. "Panties please."

She surprised him by blushing when she asked for them back. "I was hoping to keep them as a souvenir." He pretended to pout, but dug in his pocket and held the scrap of lace out. He straightened his clothes and she pushed the panties back at him. He tucked them back into his pocket and watched Alex and smooth her skirt into place. Clothing repaired, he cuddled her close to his side and kissed her gently.

Lost for something to say, Alex thanked him, and added, "I enjoyed that immensely." Her handed brushed something small and round on the seat, she picked it up. His button! She slipped it into her skirt pocket with a smug smile. He had really wanted her and this was her proof, her memento of this wild night.

She looked up and the cabbie met her eye in the mirror. He raised his eyebrow and grinned at her, she grinned back. She knew that her ardent response should have embarrassed her, but it didn't. Joe's presence and his touch had moved her more than any man ever had. He had given her some of the best orgasms of her life and she wasn't ashamed of that. She tipped her face towards Joe, kissed his cheek and cupped his hand where is rested against her shoulder. Yes indeed, there was something special about this man and his effect on her.

A few short moments later, the cab slowed to a stop outside a brightly lit café. "Here we are folks. Gina's makes the best coffee and pie in town."

"What do we owe you?" Joe asked battling a bit of chagrin at their antics and their inability to resist each other.

"Mr. you've got yourself one special woman there. You don't owe me anything. Not one red cent," the cabbie chuckled. "That was one hell of a trip and a damned fine night's entertainment. You're lucky I didn't crash the car trying to get a better look. You folks can ride in my cab anytime. No charge." He handed Joe a business card.

Joe started laughing and Alex laughed with him. She groaned and buried her face in her hands as she slid out of the car, Joe following quickly behind her.

"You folks try the pie, but keep your clothes on. Gina's not as forgiving as I am," he called through his open window of the cab. Laughing, he gave them a jaunty wave and sped away.

Trying to still her laughter, Alex leaned into Joe. His arm slid around her shoulders and he cuddled her into his side. When he leaned down to kiss her on the nose, her heart skipped a beat and she grinned up at Joe. She was glad she met him tonight. "Are going to buy me a piece of that pie Joe Brooks?" She asked. "Because, I've worked up quite an appetite." She grinned and winked at him.

Joe smiled back at Alex, and taking her hand, he led her into the cafe. "I'll buy you all the pie you can eat." He kissed her gently on the top of her head. "That cabbie sure had it right. You, Just Alex, you are once special lady, and tonight has been one wild ride."

Love the story you just read?

Your opinion matters.

Review this book on your favorite book site, review site, blog, or your own social media properties, and share your opinion with other readers.
Thanks in advance. Katie.

Other Books by Katie

Contemporary Romance Series
Heart's Haven (Resplendence Publishing)
Running Home
Saving Grace
Building Trust

Contemporary Romance Single Title
To a Tea
Rekindled Fire
Hearts in the Spotlight

Erotic Romance/Erotica

Stand Alone Erotic Romances
Tessa's Trio
The Gift

Covet the Cowboy Erotic Romance Series
Corralling the Cowboy (Book 1)
Cornering the Cowgirl (Book 2)

About Katie O'Connor

Katie O'Connor lives in Calgary, Alberta, Canada. She married her high school sweetheart and is living her happily ever after. She is the mother of two grown daughters and is extremely proud of her five grandchildren. She has two wonderful sons-in-law and a large support network of friends, family and fellow authors.

Katie's career path has been long and twisted, with most of her life devoted to her family. She's been a waitress, chambermaid, cashier, store manager, as well as a lab and x-ray technician. She is an avid quilter and crafter.

She's dabbled in writing since high school because something drives her to create stories. She swears that it's impossible for her NOT to write. Unsatisfied with one genre, Katie writes contemporary romance, erotic romance and erotica. Recently, she's crafted her first cozy mystery with the intention of publishing a cozy mystery series.

She believes in all things magical; including dragons, fairies, UFOs, ghosts, and house pixies. But most of all she believes in love, romance and hope.

Katie likes to make it up as she goes along and dreams of publishing a mixed genre novel. It is going to be an erotic, shape shifter, vampire, steampunk, sci-fi, murder mystery, adventure, romantic, western, historical, thriller. It will be her biography.

Contact Katie O'Connor

Katie loves to hear from her readers. Feel free to contact her anytime.

Website: https://katieohwrites.com
Email: katieoconnorwrites@gmail.com
Facebook: http://www.facebook.com/katieohwrites

Reviews are an author's life blood.
To thank readers generous enough to leave a review, I hold a monthly draw for a free e-book.
To enter, simply email me the link to your review.
(katieoconnorwrites@gmail.com)
Each month's winner will receive the e-book of her choice from Katie's publications.

Thank you in advance, Katie.

www.ingramcontent.com/pod-product-compliance
Lightning Source LLC
Chambersburg PA
CBHW020344130626
46549CB00003B/1279